Where's my sock, Mack?

An Ivy and Mack story

Written by Juliet Clare Bell

Illustrated by Gustavo Mazali

Collins

Who and what is in this story?

Listen and say 🎧①

pillow

Ivy

Mack

Croc

picture

ruler

Download the audio at www.collins.co.uk/839744

sock

Ivy says, "Mack? Where's my sock?"

Mack says, "Croc says you are wearing it."

Ivy says, "Not *THIS* one!"

Mack says, "Is it in my bedroom?"

Ivy says, "I don't know, Mack. *Is* it in your bedroom?"

Mack says, "Let's look."

7

Mack says, "Croc says, 'is it under my pillow?' "

Ivy says, "I don't know, Croc. *Is* it under your pillow?"

9

Mack says, "*Look* at it."
Ivy says, "It's a sock."

Mack says, "A *beautiful* sock."

11

Ivy says, "Would you like my sock, Mack?"

13

Ivy says, "Would you like *this* sock, too?"

Mack says, "No, thank you, Ivy. I like this one. *This* sock is my favourite."

Ivy says, "What things are under your pillow?"

Mack says, "My *favourite* things!"

Ivy says, "But look at the picture … !"

17

Mack says, "Yes, I know! It's very beautiful. It's my *favourite* picture!"

Ivy says, "But how do you *sleep*?"

Mack says, "Very well. Croc does, too.
Thank you for the sock, Ivy.
I am very happy."

Ivy says, "Me too. Good night, Mack."

Picture dictionary

Listen and repeat

favourite

picture

pillow

ruler

sleep

sock

1 Look and order the story

2 Listen and say

Collins

Published by Collins
An imprint of HarperCollins*Publishers*
Westerhill Road
Bishopbriggs
Glasgow
G64 2QT

HarperCollins*Publishers*
1st Floor, Watermarque Building
Ringsend Road
Dublin 4
Ireland

William Collins' dream of knowledge for all began with the publication of his first book in 1819.

A self-educated mill worker, he not only enriched millions of lives, but also founded a flourishing publishing house. Today, staying true to this spirit, Collins books are packed with inspiration, innovation and practical expertise. They place you at the centre of a world of possibility and give you exactly what you need to explore it.

© HarperCollins*Publishers* Limited 2020

10 9 8 7 6 5 4 3 2

ISBN 978-0-00-839744-9

Collins® and COBUILD® are registered trademarks of HarperCollins*Publishers* Limited

www.collins.co.uk/elt

British Library Cataloguing in Publication Data

A catalogue record for this publication is available from the British Library.

Author: Juliet Clare Bell
Illustrator: Gustavo Mazali (Beehive)
Series editor: Rebecca Adlard
Publishing manager: Lisa Todd
Product managers: Jennifer Hall and Caroline Green
In-house editor: Alma Puts Keren
Project manager: Emily Hooton
Editor: Deborah Friedland
Proofreaders: Natalie Murray and Michael Lamb
Cover designer: Kevin Robbins
Typesetter: 2Hoots Publishing Services Ltd
Audio produced by id audio, London
Reading guide author: Julie Penn
Production controller: Rachel Weaver
Printed and bound by: GPS Group, Slovenia

Download the audio for this book and a reading guide for parents and teachers at www.collins.co.uk/839744